How Amusement Parks Work

Lisa Greathouse

How Amusement Parks Work

Publishing Credits

Editorial Director
Dona Herweck Rice

Associate Editors
James Anderson
Torrey Maloof

Editor-in-Chief
Sharon Coan, M.S.Ed.

Creative Director
Lee Aucoin

Illustration Manager
Timothy J. Bradley

Publisher
Rachelle Cracchiolo, M.S.Ed.

Science Consultant
Scot Oschman, Ph.D.

Teacher Created Materials
5301 Oceanus Drive
Huntington Beach, CA 92649-1030
http://www.tcmpub.com

ISBN 978-1-4333-0308-1

Printed by: 51497
Printed in: China

Table of Contents

The Science of Amusement Parks

Have you ever been to an amusement park? Millions of people visit these fun parks every year. Not many people think about science while there. But amusement parks would not exist without science! In fact, you could think of an amusement park as one big science lab.

Do you wonder how amusement park rides work? What keeps the roller coaster on its track? How does the free-fall ride stop? What keeps the Ferris wheel steady?

Mechanics (muh-KAN-iks) can answer most of these questions. Mechanics is the type of science that deals with **motion**. Most people who design rides are **engineers** (en-juh-NEERS). Engineers are people who study mechanics.

Disneyland became the first modern theme park when it opened in Anaheim, California, in 1955.

Older Than You Think!

Amusement parks are more than 500 years old! Pleasure Gardens in Europe began in the 1500s. They had rides, games, and music. New York's Coney Island was North America's first amusement park in the 1870s. The modern theme park began in 1955. That is when Walt Disney opened Disneyland.

Simple and Compound Machines

inclined plane

You might not think of rides as machines. But that is exactly what they are. People use machines to make life easier and more fun.

There are six kinds of **simple machines.** They are the lever, the **inclined plane**, the wedge, the screw, the pulley, and the wheel and axle. They make it easier to move things.

An inclined plane is really just a ramp. Think about carrying a heavy box up some stairs. Sliding the box up the ramp makes it easier to move the box. It is also easier to roll a heavy box on a wagon than it is to carry it. The wagon uses the wheel and axle.

Compound machines are made of simple machines that work together. They can do harder jobs than simple machines alone can do. Just about every machine you see is a compound machine. That includes all the rides at an amusement park!

Ferris Wheel

The Ferris wheel is a great example of the wheel and axle in action. The structure of a Ferris wheel can be compared to two bicycle tires. The wheels are connected to the axle by spokes. Motors keep the wheels in motion. They turn a series of gears, belts, and pulleys that are all connected to one another.

Compound machines in action!

Round and Round

The Ferris wheel was invented by bridge builder George W. Ferris. The first one opened in 1893 at the Chicago World's Fair.

A Force of Nature

Isaac Newton was one of the most famous scientists in history. He was very good at using math to describe forces he saw in nature. The math used to figure out how things move is named after him. It is called Newtonian Mechanics.

Isaac Newton

When the cue stick hits the pool balls, it sets off a chain reaction of force and motion. That is Newton's Laws of Motion in action.

Everything Moves

Everything moves. Earth moves around the sun. Plants grow. Cells in living things move. Amusement park rides move for sure! But the rides do not move by themselves. **Force** is needed for any object to move. Force involves a push, pull, or twist.

Newton's Laws of Motion

One of the most famous scientists to study motion was Isaac Newton. He lived in the 1600s. His work led to laws about the way things move. They are called Newton's Laws of Motion. Engineers must know these laws to design amusement park rides.

The first law says that an object at rest will stay at rest if there is no outside force to put it into motion. It also says that a moving object will keep moving at the same speed and in the same direction unless something gets in the way. So if you hit a pool ball with a cue stick and nothing gets in its way, it just keeps rolling until friction slows it down.

The same is true for a bumper car. Without something to stop it, it will just keep going. Without something to start it, it will stay at rest.

Newton's second law explains what happens when you apply a force to an object. The object speeds up or slows down. The greater the force, the more the object speeds up or slows down.

Think about that bumper car. The harder the car is hit from behind, the more it will move forward. The heavier the object, the bigger the force must be to move it. That means a heavy bumper car would need more force to move it than a lighter one would.

Newton's third law says that when a force pushes on an object, the object pushes back in the opposite direction. Think back to the bumper cars. The car that hits yours also feels a jolt. It will stop. And it may move backwards. That is because the car reacts to the force of your car.

Newton's Laws can all be seen in the activity of bumper cars.

What Goes Up, Must Come Down

Another kind of force that keeps things in motion is **gravity** (GRAV-uh-tee). Gravity is the force that pulls everything toward Earth. It keeps your feet on the ground!

Gravity is also the force used in a free-fall ride. Motors bring riders to the top of the tower. But the exciting part of the ride is based on gravity. With their feet dangling, the riders drop fast! The ride comes to gentle stops in stages. If it zoomed down all at once, riders might be hurt.

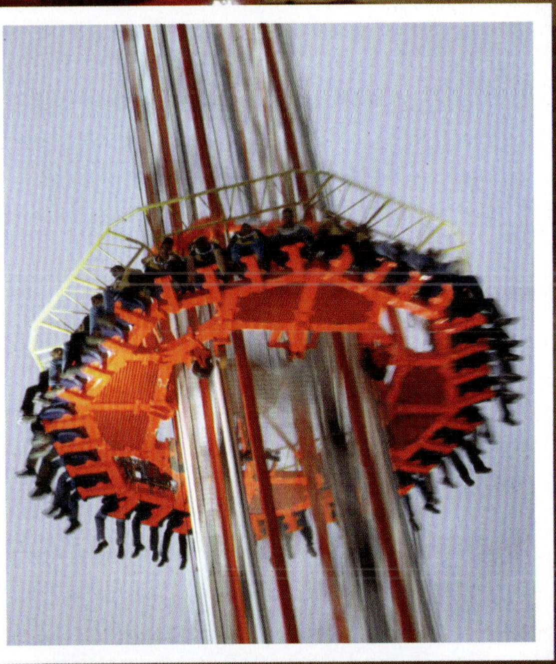

Measuring Motion

Engineers who design rides must be able to measure motion. They need to know how fast the ride will go. This will keep the riders safe.

People who drive must also be able to measure motion. Cars measure things like distance, speed, and time. If they did not, we would not know how far or how fast we drive.

There are many ways we can measure an object's motion. One way is by measuring its **speed**. Speed is how fast the object is moving. In the same amount of time, a car moving fast will cover more distance than a slower-moving car.

Ready, set, go! To figure out the speed of anything, divide the distance traveled by the time it took to travel that far.

Carousels

Carousels are not as exciting as other rides at the amusement park. But they rely on the laws of motion, too. It may seem simple, but all the horses on a carousel must move through one complete circle in the same amount of time.

Fastest Roller Coasters*

Rank	Roller Coaster	Speed	Location
1.	Ring Racer	217 kph/135 mph	Nürburgring, Rhineland-Palatinate, German
2.	Kingda Ka	206 kph/128 mph	Six Flags Great Adventure, New Jersey, U.S.A.
3.	Top Thrill Dragster	193 kph/120 mph	Cedar Point, Ohio, U.S.A.
4.	Dodonpa	172 kph/107 mph	Fuji-Q Highland, Yamanashi, Japan
5. (tie)	Superman: The Escape	161 kph/100 mph	Six Flags Magic Mountain, California, U.S.A.
5. (tie)	Tower of Terror	161 kph/100 mph	Dreamworld, Queensland, Australia

* According to Roller Coaster Database

Velocity and Acceleration

Another way to measure motion is called **velocity** (vuh-LOS-uh-tee). This is how an object's position changes over time. Velocity is a change in speed and direction. Think about jogging in place. You might be moving your legs very fast. But in the end your place has not changed. So, that would be zero velocity.

Another measurement is **acceleration**. (ak-sel-uh-RAY-shuhn). Many people think acceleration means moving fast. But a person can be moving fast and still not accelerate. An object accelerates if it changes speed. If a ride begins to move forward, that is acceleration. When it slows down, it is negative acceleration. That is called **deceleration** (dee-sel-uh-REY-shuhn).

Kingda Ka at Six Flags is 139 meters (456 feet) high!

Thrills and Chills

Some people travel all over the world to visit amusement parks. They wait hours in line for short rides. Why do they do it? For many people, it is all about the roller coaster. There is good reason why some people call it the "scream machine." The people who design roller coasters are always looking for ways to add more thrills and chills.

What makes one roller coaster more exciting than another? Some people would say that it is how steep the drops are. Other people would say it is the speed. But most roller coasters do not go much faster than cars on the freeway. Acceleration is what makes it feel so fast. Some new roller coasters can reach top speeds in just two seconds!

The wooden Cyclone roller coaster in New York's Coney Island is a landmark.

Wooden vs. Steel

Some people like steel roller coasters. Others prefer ones made of wood. If you are looking for the biggest acceleration, you will want to go with steel. Wooden roller coasters are usually not as tall or as fast as steel ones are. Most wooden ones also do not have loops. So why do so many thrill seekers love wooden coasters? It is because the wood makes the coaster sway a lot more. Now *that's* scary!

The word "kinetic" is from the Greek word meaning "to move."

The Big Drop

No matter how many loops or turns a roller coaster has, one thing is for sure: The first hill is always the highest. That is because the coaster relies on the energy from that first drop to power it through the rest of the ride. The top of the first hill is called the stop height. That is the height from which the coaster is set in motion, and it can never go higher than the stop height.

Potential and Kinetic Energy

Roller coasters do not have engines like cars have. When the ride begins, the cars are pulled up to the top of the first hill by a motor. But when they get to the top of the first hill, the cars do the rest on their own.

At that point, they have **potential** (puh-TEN-shuhl) **energy**. That means the energy is stored. It is caused by its position. All objects in high places have potential energy. Gravity takes over at the top of the hill. It keeps the cars on the tracks as they zoom down hills, turns, and loops. The potential energy changes to **kinetic** (ki-NET-ik) **energy** as the coaster goes down the hill. That is the energy of motion. Each time the coaster goes up another hill, the kinetic energy becomes potential energy again. The cycle continues again and again.

Air brakes stop the roller coaster at the end of the ride. They are built right into the track. They are *definitely* one of the most important parts of the ride.

That Sinking Feeling

There are some people who will not go on any rides with big dips or loops. They do not like the way these rides make them feel. You feel it with your whole body when a roller coaster accelerates fast. All of your body parts are pushed around. Then there is the feeling you get when the ride roars down a steep hill. That weightless feeling is the effect of gravity.

Normally, all the parts of your body are pushing on each other. That is because of the force of gravity. When you drop down a hill, all your body parts shift. Some people say it feels as if their stomachs jumped to their mouths!

The Feeling of Danger

When a roller coaster takes off fast, you really are glued to your seat! You might feel like you are going to fly off the track during hairpin turns and death-defying loops. But believe it or not, you are safer on a roller coaster than you are in your car on the road. The designers of the ride want you to feel like you are in danger. But the rides are really very safe.

Engineers follow safety standards when designing rides to keep you safe, even if you do not always feel safe.

Free Fall

You also get that weightless feeling on a free-fall ride. Free-fall rides have three parts. First, a motor takes the ride to the top. Then there are a few seconds when the ride is held in the air. Finally, there is the downward drop. The potential energy that was stored at the top turns into kinetic energy.

The force that keeps you inside the car works against gravity. The two forces cancel each other out. This creates that feeling of weightlessness. It is also called **zero gravity**. You feel like you are going to crash to the ground. But that is what makes the ride so exciting! Of course, you do not crash. Brakes slow you down. You come to a safe stop at the bottom.

Space Ride

Free-fall machines were originally made so that astronauts could experience zero gravity before going into space.

That Queasy Feeling

Some people who go on pendulum rides get a feeling that is like being seasick. And it is not because the ride is in the shape of a boat! Motion sickness is caused when the information from your eyes does not match your inner ear's ability to sense motion.

Keep your eyes closed or focus on a nonmoving, faraway point to avoid motion sickness.

Pendulum Rides

It might seem strange for people to wait in long lines for just a huge swing. But the pendulum (PEN-juh-luhm) ride is very popular.

Most pendulum rides have big open areas with seats. One example is the pirate ship ride. The ride has an arm attached to an axle. One end of the arm holds the ship. The other has a heavy weight. A motor makes the ship swing back and forth. The ship goes higher and higher. It builds **momentum** (moh-MEN-tuhm). Momentum is speed. The ship swings so high that riders think it will go upside down. In fact, some pendulum rides do go in a full circle. When it turns upside down, riders get that feeling of being weightless again!

Don't lose your lunch! Your insides shift when experiencing zero gravity. Make sure not to eat a big meal before riding a pendulum!

a virtual reality ride in Japan

Rides of the Future

In the future, there may be rides made just for you! Designers are putting some elements from video games into their rides. Then riders with different skills will have different experiences.

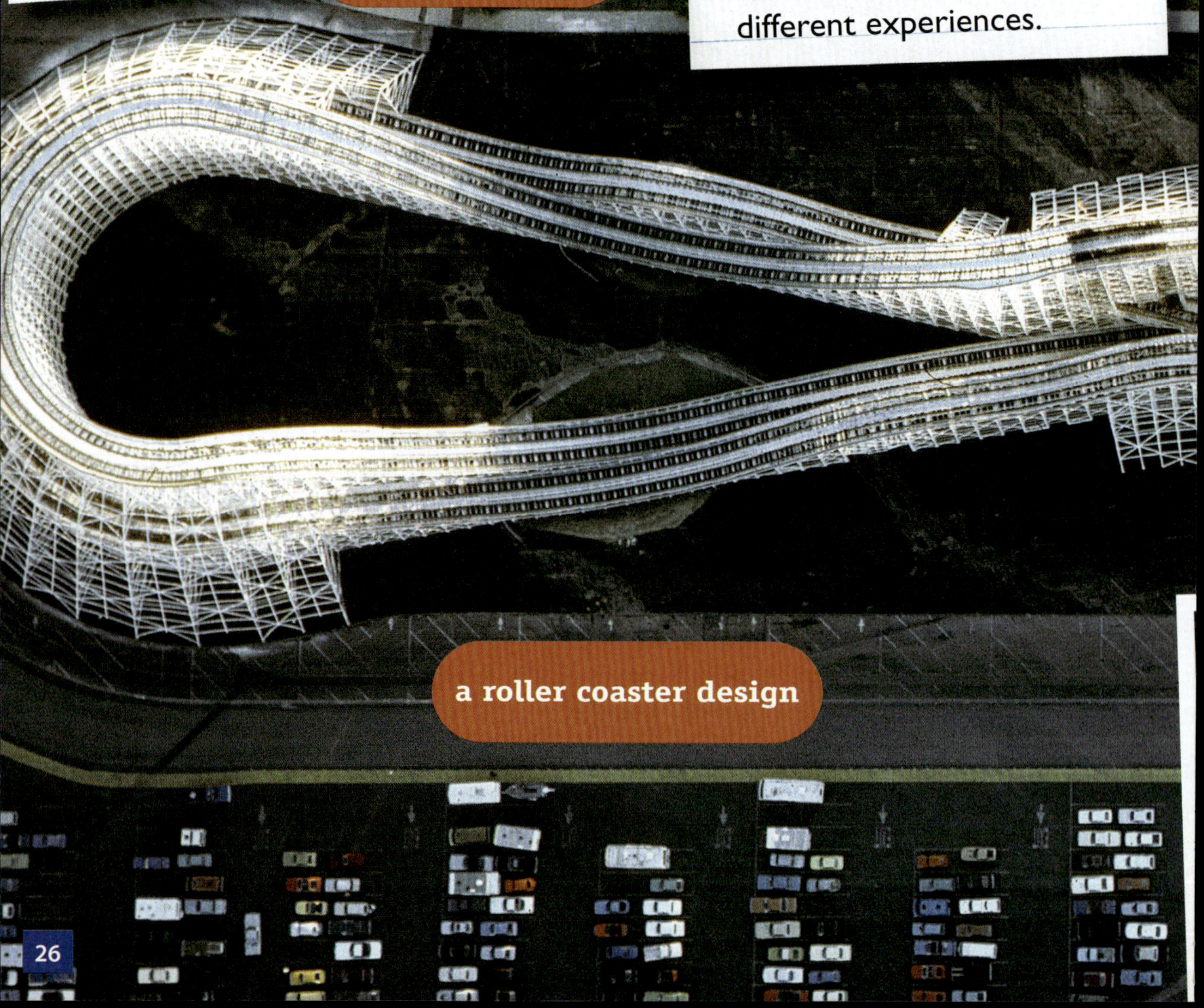

a roller coaster design

Will *You* Build the Next Great Ride?

Do you love amusement parks? Do you have an idea for a thrilling ride? Most people who design rides study engineering. Many study math. They are also very creative.

Designing a ride takes teamwork. Rides are designed on paper first. Then models are made. Engineers work with artists and **architects** (ar-ki-TECTS). Architects draw the plans for building things. Different kinds of engineers must work together.

Engineers are problem solvers. Their goal is to make rides as exciting and fun as they can be while keeping riders safe.

Engineers work on a robotic figure for a new ride.

Lab: Make Your Own Pinwheel

A pinwheel is an example of a simple machine. It is basically a wheel and an axle. A pinwheel uses wind as an energy source to make it spin.

Materials

- a sharpened pencil
- scissors
- white construction paper
- ruler
- a paper fastener
- a plastic drinking straw
- crayons, colored pencils, or markers

Procedure:

1. Cut a piece of construction paper into a 17.5 cm x 17.5 cm (7 inch by 7 inch) square.
2. Decorate both sides of the paper with crayons, markers, or colored pencils.
3. Place a ruler diagonally from one corner of the square to the opposite corner. Follow the diagonal line of the ruler and draw a 7.5 cm (3 inch) line toward the middle. Repeat this for each corner, so that you have four lines drawn toward the middle.

4. Draw a small circle to the left of each line, near the edge of the paper.

5. Cut along each line, but try not to cut all the way into the center.

6. Pull each corner into the center and make the four circles meet at the center of the square.

7. Push the end of the paper fastener through the circles. Push the fastener through the center.

8. Use the sharpened pencil to poke a hole through the straw that is about 1.25 cm (.5 inch) from the top.

9. Place the straw on the backside of your pinwheel and push the ends of the fastener through the hole in the straw. Open the fastener by flattening the ends in opposite directions.

10. Now all you need is a little breeze to make your new pinwheel spin.

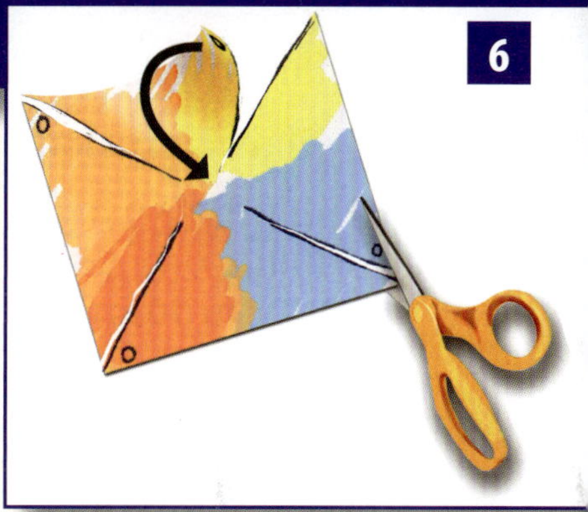

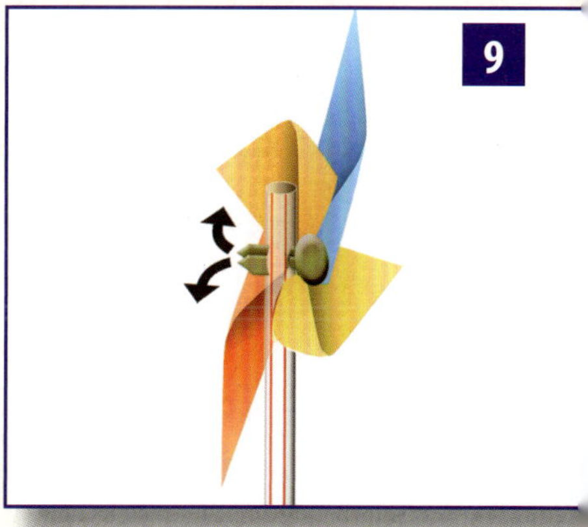

Glossary

acceleration—a change in speed

architect—a person who designs buildings or other structures

compound machine—two or more simple machines working together

deceleration—a reduction in speed

engineer—a person who plans, builds, or manages a project

force—a push or pull that makes things move

gravity—force that attracts things to each other

inclined plane—a simple machine for elevating objects

kinetic energy—the energy of motion

mechanics—a branch of science that deals with motion

momentum—force or speed of movement

motion—a change in position

potential energy—stored energy

simple machine—a machine that uses one movement to make work easier

speed—how fast something moves

velocity—the rate of change of position over time

zero gravity—no gravity; weightlessness

Index

Scientists Then and Now

Augusta Ada King, Countess of Lovelace (1815–1852)

Countess Lovelace is best known for thinking up the "analytical engine." It was an early model computer. She wrote a complete set of instructions for the engine. Her instructions are considered to be the world's first computer program!

Chavon Grande (1978–)

Chavon Grande is an engineer. Engineers design and build things. Amusement park rides are just one type of thing that Grande has made! Today, she designs many kinds of structures. One of her main jobs is to be sure that the structures protect and respect the environment.

Image Credits

Cover Sergey I/Shutterstock; p.1 Sergey I/Shutterstock; p.3-4(top) Petr Nad/Shutterstock; p.3-4(bottom) Hulton Archive/Getty Images; p.6-7(top) David R. Frazier/Photo Researchers, Inc.; p.6-7 Racheal Grazias/Shutterstock; p.7 The Granger Collection, New York; p.8 B. Sanerson/Photo Researchers, Inc.; p.8-9 terekhov igor/Shutterstock; p.10-11 Newscom; p.11 Herbert Kehrer/zefa/Corbis; p.11 jaddingt/Shutterstock; p.12-13 Filip Fuxa/Shutterstock; p.12 Juriah Mosin/Shutterstock; p.14-15 iStockphoto; p.15 Six Flags / Splash News/Newscom; p.16(top) Randy Faris/Corbis; p.16 ZUMA Press/Newcom; p.16-17 Getty Images; p.18-19 Jupiterimages Corporation; p.18-19(small) Kenneth Denton; p.20-21 WizData, Inc./Shutterstock; p.21 NASA; p.22 Charles O. Cecil/Alamy; p.22-23 Ted Pink/Alamy; p.24 Getty Images; p.24-25 Alamy; p.25 Alamy; p.26-27 Georg Gerster/Photo Researchers, Inc.; p.26-27(top) Michael S. Yamashita/CORBIS; p.27 J. Emilio Flores/The New York Times/Redux; p.29 kazberry/Shutterstock; p.32(left) National Physical Gallery, Teddington; p.32(right) Rick Reason